I0536526

ALSO BY THOMAS PRIDE

Fever

Mercia

The Baron

Wonderful Untouchables

Zayed

King and Country

THOMAS PRIDE

Ucadia Books Company

King and Country. Copyright © 2018 by Thomas Pride. All rights reserved.

No part of this book may be reproduced, or stored in a retrieval system, or transmitted in any form or by any means electronic, mechanical, photocopying, recording or otherwise, without the express and authentic written permission of the publisher.

All names, characters, organisations, places, events or incidents in this publication are fictitious or used fictitiously. Any resemblance to real persons, living or deceased, or actual events is purely coincidental.

Published by Ucadia Books Company, a Delaware stock corporation (File Number 6779670) 901 N Market St #705 Wilmington Delaware 19801. First edition.

Thomas Pride is the pen name and true ancestor of an Australian based philosopher and writer.

ISBN 978-1-64419-001-2

Our Home as our Kingdom

For many of us, our home and community is our kingdom. Sure, there is the pomp and ceremony of those few people actually called monarchs - but for the rest of us, our streets, our parks and our homes are the centre of our universe.

So what would happen if such a place was under threat - not by the forces of nature but the financial greed of others? How would we react? Would we defend our rights? Could we succeed?

Even though we live in different places and represent many cultures, we all share a common bond. This is the story of a small, sleepy seaside holiday town that awoke to face such a challenge.

To Blondie, Ms Kissy and Auggie.

Everything I know I learned from dogs.

Nora Roberts

Chapter 1

A warm and breezy seaside afternoon. An Australian Shepherd dog negotiated his way along an overgrown paved pathway, a white envelope gripped firmly in his mouth. A figure wearing a pair of old tennis shoes shuffled a few steps behind. The dog stepped up onto a front patio in front of a blue door.

"Drop it Rex."

The voice had an unmistakable American accent as Rex dutifully dropped the envelope with the name *Kate* written on its front. The figure in tennis shoes nudged the envelope further under the blue door.

"Good boy."

An older tanned hand reached down to pat Rex on the head. The figure of Percy Hamilton in all his glory is revealed - a late middle aged American, well past his prime, yet still wearing a faded Hawaiian shirt and Havanas. Percy closed the gate at the end of the path after Rex. They continued walking along the footpath for a few more steps, before stopping. Gazing ahead, they surveyed the sleepy seaside town of Eelang.

****

Along the Main Street of Eelang, Percy and Rex walked past the handful of shops and businesses at the pace of a funeral procession. They shuffled past a dilapidated two pump service station (Koz Motors). There, a scruffy looking Eastern European man (Koz), with a cigarette hanging out of his mouth, was putting out a sign. Koz smiled at Rex, but ignored eye contact with Percy, instead walking back into the office.

Further along, Percy and Rex crept past a fidgety figure (Harry Feldon) gangling a set of keys outside a store named Eelang News & Souvenirs. At first Harry Feldon seemed preoccupied with discovering the correct key from his bundle, before glancing sideways and spotting Percy and Rex. He too smiled at Rex, before revealing a darting look of contempt at Percy. Harry Feldon then flicked back to gangling and obsessing over finding the correct store key.

A bit further along and on the same side of the street as the service station, an older apron wearing Chinese woman (Vivien Li), continued to assemble an assortment of goods out the front of Eelang General Store. She curled up her face in disgust at Percy, who equally ignored her to fix his gaze straight ahead. Just as Percy and Rex pass her by, Vivien Li quickly reached into the pocket of her apron and produced a treat for Rex, who grabbed it, swallowed it in one gulp and then returned to the side of Percy.

On the opposite side of the road, a beer truck had pulled up out the front of the Eelang Arms Hotel, where Alexia Aristis was directing the unloading of barrels into the basement. Further along, was as an old man (Bart Manning) in a faded tweed jacket and pants sitting on a chair next to the side of the hotel, half asleep. Alexia looked up as Percy and Rex passed on the other side of the road and shook her head negatively at them as Percy continued his walk of shame.

****

Rex began relieving himself against one of the supports of a giant billboard at the edge of town.

"I know Rex," groaned Percy. "I should have listened to you."

The dog finished relieving itself against the side of the billboard. As they walked away, the content of the billboard was revealed. A giant defaced picture of Percy along with a defaced picture of a man in Mayoral Robes (Barry Bruce) in front of an image of a new Marina and multi-storey hotel. At the top of the billboard was the slogan *New Eelang Resort And Marina* and the symbol of Omnibank. Someone has also spray painted the words Traitor and Sell Out across the billboard.

****

Percy sat bare foot with Rex on a grassy headland, looking out toward the ocean. For a moment, Percy closed his eyes and let the sea breeze and sun brush his face. He slowly opened his eyes and turned around to pat Rex.

"It looks like it is time Rex."

Chapter 1

Rex looked at him sheepishly as Percy stood up and walked closer to the edge of the grassy headland. The moment was interrupted by the sound of an approaching car horn blaring. A dilapidated old model Mercedes - with a Taxi light and signs called *Eelang Premier Cabs* was being driven up the headland road toward Percy. The cab beeped its horn twice more before abruptly stopping. A woman (Kate) with a clearly annoyed look on her face leapt out of the cab. She marched toward the grassy headland and the location of Percy.

"What kind of perverse stunt are you trying to pull this time Percy?"

Percy ignored her, as he still looked out at the ocean. "I mean it Kate. What is the point?"

"So, what you are going to do? Break a leg or your hip for sympathy?"

Percy responded with a look of confusion before Kate stepped forward. She grabbing his left hand in frustration and pulled him to the very edge, pointing to the sea below.

"It's ten feet Percy. And the tide is in."

Indeed, the headland was only a few feet above the sea, with the water lapping the rocky edge at high tide.

Percy sat down defeated, with his legs over the edge. Rex the dog came up and sat beside him suitably melancholy - as if on queue, while Kate remained standing.

"What can I do? The whole town hates me," he sighed.

"What do you expect? You and Barry Bruce gave Eelang away to a bunch of greedy bankers. The town named after my great grandfather."

Percy put his head in his hands. "I know and I hate myself for trusting Barry Bruce."

Kate put her hand on the back of Percy and then sat down next to him. "Who knows where our mayor has run off to with all that money? But thinking of killing yourself isn't the answer."

"But - "

"Percy, the whole town saw you. You walked here. You never walk. And besides, you left me your cab and keys and a note, so don't give me that crap."

Percy shrugged his shoulders. "So what do I do?"

Kate looked out at the ocean as the sun and breeze touched her face. In a moment of calm she turned back to look at Percy.

"I'm flying to the city in a couple of days for a court hearing to try and stop this. But in the meantime you can start by helping me finish the posters for the protest rally at the construction site. We have a reporter coming at midday."

"Do you really think it will make a difference?"

"We can try can't we?"

"Percy you've made a big mess. Don't leave it for someone else to fix it all."

Percy nodded sheepishly.

Chapter 2

It was morning at Kate's House in an older open style kitchen. Kate and her teenage children (Sophie and Ben), as well as Percy and another woman (Mary-Ann), were standing around a wooden kitchen table, making signs and attaching them to wooden stakes.

"Hey mum, what do you think?" said Ben proudly, holding a protest poster with the slogan BANKS SUCK YOU!

Kate looked at the poster and then at Mary-Ann, who after glancing the finished poster of Ben, seemed to struggle to keep her composure.

"Honey, its -"

Before Kate could finish, Harry Feldon, from the Eelang News & Gift Shop, bounced into the kitchen, carrying a dozen more pieces of white board.

"That's all of the stock," he pronounced breathlessly.

Harry surveyed the people in the kitchen, first acknowledging and smiling at Kate, Mary-Ann, Sophie, then Ben and finally the poster of Ben. Instantly, Harry burst into a giggle fit, causing Mary-Ann to also crack and lose her composure and join in. Then Harry saw Percy standing away at a side bench behind Kate, using a marker pen to write signs. His laughter evaporated.

"You!" he screamed.

"Now, Harry this is not the time," said Kate.

"I live here too, remember!" replied Percy.

"No you don't!" added Ben, unhelpfully. "You live in our backyard."

"But, but," spluttered Harry, "he is the whole reason -"

Kate put her hand up at Harry to stop, then looked at Ben. "Ben, honey, I think you mixed the words around the wrong way."

"No I didn't, I mean it," said Ben indignantly.

"I am just trying to help -" protested Percy.

"Help! You could help by drowning yourself," added Harry. "That would be a tremendous help -"

"Everyone," shouted Kate, "shut up!"

Sudden silence in the kitchen. Kate looked at Percy and pointed a finger at him.

"Percy, go and get the rest of the tape in the dining room, next to the finished posters."

Percy dutifully shuffled out of the room. Kate turned her attention to Harry.

"Harry thank you! You can take the finished placards and we will see you down at the building site in the next hour, OK?"

Harry Feldon nodded and scampered away. Meanwhile, in the adjoining dining room that seemed to have been renovated sometime in the late 1980's, Percy looked for the rolls of tape. He found them sitting on a sofa positioned in front of a portrait of a stern looking man (Charles E. Lang), his name attached to a nameplate at the bottom of the portrait.

Percy stared at the portrait for a moment. He seemed to shiver, before hurrying back to the kitchen.

In the kitchen, Percy handed Kate the tape.

"Thanks," she smiled. "Now go and help Harry load the finished signs."

"But you heard him," said Percy, "he wants me to drown myself."

"So he is a saint compared to what the others want to do to you. Get over yourself Percy."

Percy shrugged his shoulders and left to follow after Harry Feldon.

"And I'm not going in the dining room again," he yelled back. "I think that portrait of your great grandfather is following me."

Kate rolled her eyes as she handed another blank piece of board to Ben and Sophie to continue writing.

****

A few dozen locals with placards, including Harry Feldon, Percy, Vivian Li, Koz and Alexia Aristis were standing outside temporary fencing. Behind them, a giant sign emblazoned with the words Another Omnibank Project, with a few construction workers hemmed in on the other side of the fence.

Across the road from the building site, a TV truck with the logo *This Day Tonight on Channel 8* written across the side of the van, slowed down and parked. Soon after, a police car with its lights flashing arrived and inched its way up to the main gate of the site.

The foreman of the site smiled as he observed the police car arrive.

"Good, the cops have finally arrived."

Meanwhile, a female journalist (Susie Radcliff) and her cameraman (Russo) and sound technician (Ando) got out of the Channel 8 van.

Susie Radcliff looked at the scene across the road and turned to Russo, her cameraman. "See if you can get the police car in the shot as well," she said, and then quickly checked her make-up in the drivers side mirror.

Russo nodded as all three of the Channel 8 crew cross the road.

A tall Indigenous police officer (Sgt. Jagamara) stepped out of the police vehicle and walked toward Kate. She didn't see the police officer at first, while she remained distracted looking over at the approaching Channel 8 team.

"Is this it?" asked Sgt. Jagamara, before Kate turned around and gave him a big hug.

"Jagamara, this is the best I could do at short notice." Kate did a quick scan of familiar faces, before she smiled nervously at Jagamara. "Do you really think this will help?"

"It's all these blokes seem to respond to," replied Sgt. Jagamara, "when they risk a public punch in the face."

Susie Radcliff and her television crew spot Kate midst the crowd. Kate looked back at Sgt. Jagamara.

"The This Day Tonight crew are here, I gotta go."

Sgt. Jagamara nodded and then moved, through the placard carrying locals, over to the gates of the site. The foreman moved closer as Sgt. Jagamara stepped up to the gate.

"How can I help you boys?" smiled Sgt. Jagamara.

"Well for a start you could arrest some of these protestors on private property," said the foreman.

"How about you open the gate so we can stop talking through this grill?"

The foreman reached into his left pocket and started to fidget for a key, before opening up the gate. Sgt. Jagamara then turned around to see Kate and the Channel 8 crew walk up behind him.

"Jagamara, can you move the police car closer?" asked Kate. "The television cameraman said it is too far out of shot."

Sgt. Jagamara shrugged his shoulders, turned and started to walk back.

"No, its fine Sergeant," said Susie Radcliff. "We can get everyone in the shot. Can you just stand where you are?"

Sgt. Jagamara shrugged his shoulders again and looked back at the construction workers as Russo the cameraman set up a tripod and then placed his camera on top. Kate walked back to the protestors milling around and waved for them to start moving.

Slowly, the locals started to shuffle back and forth in front of the building site and police car, holding up their placards.

"Stop OmniBank. Save our Town. Stop the Banks. Save our Town."

Susie Radcliff then stepped in front of the camera, with the protestors and scene behind her and once Ando the sound technician gave a thumbs up, Russo the cameraman counted down with his fingers to the side, until Susie Radcliff started to speak.

"Tonight, I am reporting live from the small town of Eelang that has become the latest battleground between corporate greed of big banks versus the average community."

****

A tall skyscraper, stood out against the skyline of a big city. The clue to its main occupant being a large Omnibank sign on the front.

Inside the OmniBank Headquarters, on one of the upper floors, the Chief Executive (Ellis Pickering) of Omnibank was seated behind his desk while he watched an enormous flat screen TV on the opposite wall. The TV showed the same report on Channel 8 of Susie Radcliff at Eelang interviewing Kate Lang as the protestors move back and forth with their chant. Two other men (Martin Fay and Ed Cartwright) were also seated in the Chief Executives office watching the TV.

"So what you're saying Mrs Lang -"

"Miss Lang," interrupted Kate.

"Sorry. So what you're saying Miss Lang is that OmniBank has effectively stolen the town from underneath you, because of some corrupt mayor named Barry Bruce?"

"Yes. Yes, that's right."

"The rotten.. The horrible OmniBank stole the Marina from us and now wants to foreclose on the town to put up some huge and awful yuppie holiday resort."

Susie Radcliff turns directly to face the camera. "Thank you Ms. Lang. So there you have it. Another example of big banks stomping all over the little people."

The broadcast then cut back to a current affairs anchor (Ken Bright) frowning into the camera in front of a studio set saying This Day Tonight Channel 8 as he looks over at a Television monitor showing Susie Radcliff and her report.

The studio monitor swung back to a close up of Ken Bright still frowning sombrely.

"Susie Radcliff reporting there from the town of Eelang," he said, "where the ordinary people are struggling to survive against the big banks. I wonder what the audience thinks given the up coming federal election?"

Ellis Pickering held up a TV remote control, before he changed to another channel. The television screen now shows the smiling head of the Opposition Leader (Peter Vicar), in a campaign ad.

"You said you had this project under control?" growled Ellis Pickering.

Ed Cartwright nodded nervously as the campaign commercial continued to play in the background.

"And that is why when I am elected Prime Minister I am going to hold all the banks accountable - "

Ellis Pickering pressed the remote control again in frustration, changing the channel, only to see the tail end of another political commercial.

"So vote for Peter Vicar and I will stand up for the little guy -"

Ellis Pickering finally pressed off and threw the remote down on the desk, causing it to skid and then slide off the desk.

"And just before a Federal Election!" yelled Ellis Pickering.

"We didn't think -" said Ed Cartwright before being cut off by Ellis Pickering.

"Didn't think, exactly, that's -"

"No sir" interrupted Ed Cartwright, "We didn't anticipate this group in Eelang would be so media literate."

Ellis Pickering slapped his forehead, before looking down at his desk.

"This is the age of the Internet, for goodness sake" he sighed. "Even a twelve year old kid can download a couple of video clips and before you know it, can build a nuclear bomb or have have mastered a global news strategy."

"How do you wish us to handle it sir?"

Ellis Pickering looked out the window and then back at Ed Cartwright.

"I am sending you to Eelang personally to make sure we keep a lid on this thing and there are no more stunts like this one. Understand?"

Ed Cartwright nodded nervously.

"I want you to blend in. Don't make waves. Observe everything and make sure we know what is happening."

"I wont let you down," smiled Ed Cartwright feebly.

"For your sake let's hope this time that is true," growled Ellis Pickering.

Chapter 3

The following morning at Kate's House. In the kitchen, Sophie Lang was sitting peacefully at the island bench, eating cereal, when her mother Kate whirled in, fully dressed carrying a suitcase and looking stressfully at her wrist watch.

"Where the hell is Percy?"

Sophie shrugged her shoulders as Kate huffed and left the room. She flung open the back screen door and stepped out into the backyard. At the far end of a spacious and lush backyard was a caravan sitting under a tree. Kate looked down at Rex, still asleep next to the back door.

"Percy!" yelled Kate. "We're late."

No answer from the caravan. Kate looked back down at Rex, who now had his head up, looking at her strangely.

"Where is he Rex?"

She marched down to the caravan and flung open the door. Inside, the Caravan interior was like a tribute to the 1970's California, with Posters of The Eagles and Beachboys and surfing movies.

Kate pulled her head out the caravan and looked around, trying not to get upset.

Meanwhile, a few miles away, Percy in a wet-suit strolled out of the surf, carrying a surf board, looking every bit in his element.

****

The old Mercedes taxi of Percy was barrelling down the road, while Rex is sitting in the front seat and Kate in the back seat.

An awkward silence as Percy glanced into the rear vision mirror to see Kate, with her arms crossed, looking out the window.

"We'll make it," said Percy.

"You know I hate being late," was the reply.

A few more moments of awkward silence.

"Sorry," he added.

"Do you think you can remember, Sophie has her soccer game at 4 O'Clock?"

"4 O'Clock," said Percy.

"And no pizza for dinner! I have cooked their dinner and just take it out of the fridge."

"But Microwaves kill -"

"Percy," interrupted Kate.

The old Mercedes pulled up to a solitary building saying Eelang Airport. Kate let herself out and Percy lept out and moved around to the boot.

"So the media interview is tonight at 6.30 on Channel 4 with Angela Kostakos," she said.

"Right. Channel 4."

"And the injunction hearing to try and stop the construction is tomorrow morning," added Kate.

"Right. Got it," he said, sounding less than convincing.

Kate smiled as she leant down and kissed Rex, while Percy pulled out a small case from the boot and set its down on the footpath.

"You look after him Rex and make sure he doesn't get into any more trouble."

Kate then moved over and gave Percy a hug.

"Good luck," he said, before Kate turned and walked into the airport.

Percy stood at the entrance for a few more moments, until he could no longer see any sign of Kate.

"Excuse me," a voice said.

Percy didn't hear the voice at first.

"Excuse me, are you free?" the voice asked.

Percy snapped out of his reflective moment. He looked around at the two suited men being Ed Cartwright and Lewis Botta.

"How much to the Eelang Hotel?" asked Ed Cartwright

"Twenty dollars," said Percy nonplussed.

Ed Cartwright looked over at Lewis Botta and grinned.

"Each," added Percy.

The smile vanished from the face of Ed Cartwright as he huffed and moved to the front passenger door before spotting Rex sitting there. Rex starts to growl.

"There is a dog in the front seat," protested Ed Cartwright.

"Yes, his name is Rex. You'll have to get in the back as he doesn't like people taking his seat."

Both Ed Cartwright and Lewis Botta look at each other before they get into the car.

****

Eelang Arms Hotel

Inside, the main bar of the Eelang Arms Hotel is full with an assortment of characters, as Alexia Aristis served drinks. Percy was sitting down at one table with Sophie Lang and Ben Lang, while at another table Koz was playing cards and drinking beer with two other men (Con Poulos and Bertrone Camilleri). To the side was the lonely figure of Bart Manning drinking a beer, while in the corner Ed Cartwright and Lewis Botta in bright and new smart casual clothes were trying to blend in.

"What time is the show on?" yelled Alexia Aristis.

"6.30. Channel 4," yelled Con Poulos and Loz at the same time in reply.

Alexia pointed a television remote control toward a television set hanging above the patrons as Mary-Ann McNamara entered the main bar area carrying a pizza across to the table of Percy, Sophie and Ben.

"Kate is going to kill you," said Mary-Ann to the three of them.

"Awesome, Pizza!" said Ben enthusiastically, flipping open the lid to the pizza box.

"We were never here," said Percy to Mary-Ann, who nodded before swivelling around and eyeballing Ed Cartwright and Lewis Botta in the corner.

She whipped out an order book and smiled.

"Can I help you gentlemen?" asked Mary-Ann politely.

"That is Bullshit!" yelled Koz in the background.

"No! No it is true!" yelled Con Poulos in reply.

Mary-Ann blushed. "Sorry. The locals can be a bit loud, she said sheepishly to Ed Cartwright and Lewis Botta. "We don't really have many tourists or couples like you come through."

Ed Cartwright and Lewis Botta looked at each other before looking back at Mary-Ann, both shaking their heads.

"Oh, no we're not a couple," replied Lewis Botta, "we are -"

"Everyone shut up," shouted Alexia Aristis. "The town is on the telly."

Everyone suddenly went quiet and looked up at the television, where a female anchor (Angela Kostakos) was speaking in front of a set logo saying *Boiling Point* and the story graphic *PM Promise On Eelang Anti-Bank Protest*. Soon after the smiling figure of Prime Minister Max Wright appeared.

"That is right Angela," grinned the Prime Minister. "The government is announcing a get tough policy against anti-social bank practices."

"Like Eelang," added Angela Kostakos.

"Yes, exactly. We care for the little people, the people who are under the most pressure from the banks -"

"When sorrows come," bellowed Bart Manning in the bar, "they come not as single spies, but in battalions."

"Shut up. I can't hear," yelled Bertrone Camilleri.

"Everyone, shut up," yelled Alexia Aristis.

Bart Manning shrugged his shoulders and continued drinking his beer.

"And you are prepared to put this on the record now?" asked Angela Kostakos, "exclusively on the Boiling Point?"

"Yes. Yes I am."

"So there you have it. Exclusively and only on Boiling Point the response from the Prime Minister to the growing back lash against big banks - "

At that moment, Percy's phone began to ring.

"Shut up," yelled Bertrone Camilleri.

Percy looked down at the number and then at Sophie and Ben.

"It's your mum."

Percy got up and hurried to the door, then Percy pressed answer on the phone outside the hotel.

"Hi Kate. We just saw the television interview."

"Where are you?" she asked over the phone. "You're not at the pub are you?"

"No, I just stepped outside. The kids are good."

"Oh Percy..." she sighed.

"Kate. It is nothing to be upset about," said Percy. "They spoke about Eelang and there will be other television interviews."

Kate was sitting in a budget motel room on the phone with a set of official looking documents in front of her.

"We lost the court case," she said, her voice quivering.

"I thought that was tomorrow?"

Kate picked up the first document in her left hand while holding the phone.

"It was supposed to be and then the bank filed something called an Ex Parte Motion to strike it out because of the media and having no merit."

"How? I don't understand?" asked Percy.

Still reading the documents, before throwing it down on the ground.

"Something about vexation or frivolous or something because of the media. I don't understand it. It is all lawyer talk."

Kate started to sob. "Oh Percy, what have I done?"

"Now listen here Miss Kate Lang," said Percy sternly. "I am the one who made this mess, remember? You have done everything you could, now get some rest and I will see you tomorrow."

Kate hung up the phone and put her head in her hands. Percy put his phone away and walked back into the hotel.

As Percy walked back into the main bar, the room was deathly quiet as all eyes were on him. Percy was startled at first and looked over at Sophie and Ben. Ben shrugged his shoulders.

"I told them you were on the phone with mum."

Percy looked around at all the expectant faces.

"Alas, the world is grown so bad, that wrens make prey where eagles dare not perch," chimed Bart Manning.

"I've had about enough of your tricky words old man," growled Bertrone Camilleri."

"Shakespeare dear boy. Shakespeare -"

"Shut it Bertrone," yelled Alexia Aristis, interrupting Bart Manning. "Let's hear what our girl said from the city. That goes for you Bart. No quotes. Let Percy speak."

An eternity as Percy looked at all the expectant faces in the room, including Ed Cartwright and Lewis Botta. Percy started shaking his head negatively.

"The case is off," he said to a collective moan in the bar.

"What? That is bullshit!" erupted Koz.

Collectively mumbling as Ed Cartwright looked over at Lewis Botta who has a giant euphoric grin on his face. Ed Cartwright quickly punched him.

"Ow!" complained Lewis Botta.

Ed Cartwright pointed to the sombre look on his face and the faces of everyone else in the bar and Lewis changed his grin to a frown.

"Something about vexed motions and no merit, or something," added Percy.

"Ah, the three fates that haunt the halls of justice of scandalous, frivolous and vexatious," responded Bart Manning.

Bertrone Camilleri jumped up from the table and moved to stand menacingly over toward Bart Manning, who in turn cowered.

"Right that's it," he growled. "I'm going to knock your head off!"

"Bertrone. Sit down!" screamed Alexia Aristis. "Shut up and leave him alone."

"Dear boy, I was only talking about the tricks of the lawyers to rid themselves of the case. It is merely a game of claims and counter claims, nothing more," said Bart Manning.

"Well, whatever it is they are playing at Bart, it is my life they are messing with and our future as a town," said Alexia Aristis.

General head nodding and mumbling around the bar.

"Right. Right," added Bart Manning. "And that is the thing. It is all bluff. There is nothing to the paper. You have all the rights not them. Yet people allow themselves to be tricked into thinking they are insolvent debtors, when they can never be."

"What would you know?" laughed Koz. "You are just an old drunk that is the first into the pub and the last to leave!"

Bart Manning put down his almost empty glass of beer with a thud on the table.

"I may be a drunk that is true. But many moons ago I also used to be the finest trial lawyer in the city."

General laughter.

"Qui vult decipi decipiatur," said Bart Manning

"What did you say?" asked Koz.

"Shut up old man!" grumbled Bertrone Camilleri

"Let Him Who Wishes to be Deceived, be Deceived," replied Bart Manning.

The bar erupted with shouts of shut up and grumbling.

"Enough Bart! This is not the time," said Alexia Aristis. "Shut up with the philosophy and drink your beer."

****

Percy was kneeling uncomfortably in a confessional, his hands clenched near the closed grail, as the latch swung open. The face of the priest (Fr. Jack) was obscured by the grill of the confessional. Only the sound of his voice could be heard.

"In the name of the father and of the son...and of the holy spirit."

Percy made the sign of the cross.

"Trust in God to hear your prayers and petition," said Father Jack gently through the confessional window.

"Forgive me father, for I have made an almighty mess...I have sinned. It has been twenty, years no, ah twenty six...no that's not right, more like thirty I think..."

"So it's been a long time then Percy?"

"Yes, yes it's been too long," added Percy. "Anyway I need a miracle or something from God, so that is why I am here."

"Percy, I appreciate you letting me know about my sister Kate, but would you rather have a brief chat tomorrow and we can hear your confession a little later?"

"No. No, it has to be now."

"But Percy it is one O'Clock in the morning."

The sound of movement. "I am getting up now."

There is a click of the door to the confessional and Percy got up and let himself out. Outside, Fr. Jack was standing there in his pyjamas and wearing a stole.

"I am going to bed Percy."

"Wait Father Jack. Just one more question?"

Fr. Jack shrugged his shoulders.

"You are a priest so you know about the law and rights and stuff?"

"Sure, but I am no lawyer. Matthew 7:12 teaches us the Golden Rule of Law that all are equal and even Genesis 1 verses 26 to 29 speaks of God creating man in his image and granting him equal dominion."

"Dominion?"

"Sovereignty. That every man and woman is equal and like his own sovereign in the eyes of God."

"Ah," said Percy unconvincingly.

"That's right Percy. The Gospel has never been about binding a slave to banks. Quite the opposite. It has always been about freeing people from the evil of financial slavery."

"So what you're saying Father Jack is that I am a sovereign then? I am royalty in the eyes of the Church?"

"In a way, yes. Great Grandfather Charles E. Lang was given a land patent endorsed from England when he first formed this town. So in a sense, he was like a king of his own country back then."

Father Jack rubbed his eyes and yawned. "Anyway, I am rambling and I am tired and I am going to bed. Good night Percy."

Fr. Jack hugged Percy, then turned to walk away.

"Good night Fr. Jack."

Percy remained staring at the front altar of the church.

"And don't forget to turn off the lights when you go," yelled Father Jack.

Chapter 4

Kate arrived back on a full flight to Eelang Airport, only to discover that many of the passengers were journalists and TV crews. She even spotted Susie Radcliff leaving the building with Ken Bright from *This Day Tonight*.

Outside was a hive of activity of TV vans and cars. Kate was surprised to find Harry Feldon waiting patiently for her, next to the battered old Mercedes, instead of Percy, while a photographer was taking photos of the car.

"Where is Percy? What on earth is going on?" she asked hesitantly.

"Something brilliant!" bubbled Harry Feldon. "I promised him I would not tell until you see. Wait till you see."

Kate slapped to her forehead and sighed. "What has Percy gone and done now?"

****

Harry Feldon slowed down the Mercedes taxi opposite the Omnibank Building site. Multiple TV vans and cars had already taken up any available parking spots.

"Best if I drop you off here," he smiled.

Kate got out of the car and walked across the road to join the crowd of people as more people continued to arrive.

Kate weaved her way through the throng until she spotted her children (Sophie and Ben). Both were wearing white costumes with hats. Sophie holding a furled flag and pole. Ben holding a trumpet with a ceremonial flag underneath with only the word "EELANG" visible.

"What the hell is going on?"

Sophie shrugged her shoulders and pointed at Ben. Ben smiled sheepishly as in the distance, everyone in the crowd could hear the sound of an approaching big muscle car and a car horn playing the *Mexican Hat Dance*.

"Since when did you start playing the trumpet again?" said Kate.

"Not now mum," replied Ben. "He's coming."

The first car to approach the building site was the police car of Sgt Jagamara with its lights flashing. It was immediately followed by the familiar low growling engine sound of an open Mustang before the horn of the car blasted out the *Mexican Hat Dance* again. As the Mustang got closer, Kate could see it was Con Poulos with Koz in a white uniform next to him. Percy in a suit was sitting in the back seat waving to the people.

The crowd parted, first to make way for the police car and then the Mustang. Both cars rolled to a stop near where Kate was standing as Susie Radcliff and her crew bustled through with the other journalists to get closer.

Koz was the first to get out and quickly moved around to push the front seat forwards to allow Percy to get out. Percy caught a quick glance at Kate and smiled, but before she could say anything there was the ear piercing sound of a badly played trumpet next to her. She swung around and glared at Ben, as he mashed up an attempt at being a trumpet herald.

"Ladies and Gentlemen," said Koz. "The King of Eelang."

The sound of cameras as TV crews moved in closer and Sgt Jagamara stepped in.

"Back. Give him some space."

Percy gave Sgt Jagamara an appreciative nod as he reached into his pocket and unfolded a set of pages. Harry Feldon then appeared with a lectern and placed it in front of Percy. Percy gave Harry an appreciative smile, before Percy cleared his throat.

"Ah, thank you all for coming."

Percy paused and shuffled the pieces of paper on the wobbly lectern.

"Firstly, as some of you may have already heard, our town, the town of Eelang has been under attack from the banks after our mayor Barry Bruce ran away with a whole lot of money after doing a deal with OmniBank. Now the bank wants to come and take away our homes and our businesses and our livelihoods, all for profit."

Percy looked over at the people of Eelang standing around, watching expectantly.

"Secondly, as you may have guessed I do not have a very good Aussie accent. That is because while I was born here, my parents separated when I was still a child and I went to live with my dad in the

United States. So you see, I have always been searching for where I belong and where I fit in until I found this beautiful part of God's creation called Eelang."

Percy looked over at Kate and smiled.

"And just when I thought all was lost, someone reminded me of something every single kid who grows up in America comes to learn and memorise about our rights to our lives and our homes and our businesses: That all men are created equal, that they are endowed by their Creator with certain unalienable rights, that among these are life, liberty and the pursuit of happiness."

****

Martin Fay sprinted past secretaries toward a door marked Chief Executive Officer before swinging the door open without knocking.

Inside, Ellis Pickering was glued to the television as he turned to see Martin Fay burst in. Ellis Pickering put up his hand to Martin Fay.

"Get Cartwright on the phone NOW!" yelled Ellis Pickering.

Martin Fay nodded and opened up his mobile and started dialling.

****

In the Office of the Prime Minister in Canberra, the Prime Minister was also watching with Marion Alright the broadcast showing the continued speech of Percy.

"So you see a bank has no power to take away that which it cannot have," said Percy, "only for people to forget who and what they are and agree to some incomplete and unfair and one-sided contract. Our home is our kingdom and no one has the right to steal that from us. Nor does a bank have the right to deny the law, as possession is nine tenths of the law."

Sophie handed Percy the flag and Percy stepped out from behind the lectern and firmly plants the flag in the soil.

"That is why, in the name of all the people of Eelang," Percy added, "I declare this land sovereign and that the first act of law is to banish all banks from our land."

The Prime Minister pressed the remote and turned off the television. "What do we do now Marion?"

"The problem is that this story has struck a chord with the electorate," Marion Alight replied. "We need to contain it, before Peter Vicar and his vultures get onto it."

"Right! Get me on Boiling Point with Angela Kostakos tonight, " said the Prime Minister.

Marion Alright picked up her mobile phone and started to dial.

****

Percy stood smiling in front of the repainted and redesigned billboard, showing a beautiful picture of Eelang and a picture of Percy, with the slogan *Kingdom Of Eelang Welcomes You*. Two photographers were shooting pictures as Kate stood to the side and next to Koz. Percy looked over and recognised the impatient look on her face.

Percy signalled to Koz.

"Thank you gentlemen," said Koz. "That is all."

Percy waited for the photographers to leave and then moved closer to Kate. "Sorry, it has been an absolute blur," he smiled.

"I don't think I have ever seen you in a suit before," she responded warily. "Not even for the funeral of uncle Wally."

They both walk away from the sign, leaving Koz behind.

"Everyone is behind it 100% You should have seen their faces," said Percy.

"I did see their faces," she said sternly. "And everyone of them is scared to death they are going to lose everything. Percy, you don't have to keep pulling these kinds of stunts for people to like you. People are going to like you or hate you anyway."

"I know this all sounds crazy, but you have to trust me, this is the only way to save the town!"

Kate shook her head. "Is it? Is it Percy? Because that kind of sounds like the same thing you said to me before, except Barry Bruce was standing next to you."

Percy stepped forward as Kate recoiled back. "Kate I, I can't do this without you."

"See that is the thing Percy. I keep hoping week after week, maybe this will be the week when he says it. I Keep fooling myself, because you can't even say it."

"Say what?"

Kate shook her head negatively and turned away.

"Say what Kate? Tell me and I will say it!"

Kate continued to walk away. "If you don't get it, you never will," she yelled before leaving.

After Kate had left, Percy looked over at Koz, who shrugged his shoulders.

"I don't understand Koz," said Percy.

"My friend that is the same everywhere," grinned Koz. "It is like we are two different people."

"Yes, exactly."

"In my home country, I was a teacher with two doctorate degrees in Chemistry and Mathematics. But when I come here because of my English they said my education means nothing. So I become a mechanic."

"I never knew that Koz."

"It is not just me. You know Miss Vivien"

"The Chinese lady that is always grumpy that runs the General Store?"

Kos nodded. "She was senior Chinese Army instructor before coming to Australia."

Percy shook his head. "So why the swearing and everything I always thought -."

"Sometimes it is easier to fit so you see what you want to see. That is OK," smiled Koz. "Aussies are good. This is a nice country. You know you are American. Sometimes it is easier to let people think the way they think. And sometimes it is better to fight and say it is bullshit!"

They both laugh.

****

At the Eelang Arms Hotel, Ed Cartwright and Lewis Botta were listening to a mobile phone on speaker.

"This is the last chance Cartwright," yelled Ellis Pickering down the phone.

"Yes I fully understand sir," replied Ed Cartwright. "No more stuff ups."

"What is his name?" asked Lewis Botta, as Ed Cartwright desperately waved his hand at Lewis not to speak.

"Victor the frigging Cleaner," chuckled Ellis Pickering over the phone. "No. No. Lets just call him Winston. Mr Wolfe."

The phone line goes dead as Ed Cartwright looked nervously at Lewis Botta.

Chapter 5

The main bar of the Eelang Arms Hotel was completely jammed packed with people, as Alexia Aristis and Mary-Ann struggled to keep up. Percy was sitting down at one table with Bart Manning, Sgt Jagamara and Koz, but not really listening to the conversation.

"Everyone shut up," yelled Alexia Aristis. "They are talking about the town on the telly again."

The bar went quiet as everyone looked up at the television, where a female anchor (Angela Kostakos) was speaking in front of a logo *Boiling Point* and the story graphic *PM On Breakaway Eelang Kingdom*.

The figure of a smiling Prime Minister Max Wright then appeared on camera.

"So what you are saying Prime Minister is that the people of Eelang are missing the point?"

"Exactly Angela. Look, I don't like the way the banks behave just as much as the average voter, but the law is the law. And every citizen is a sovereign in a sense."

"A Sovereign Citizen?"

"Right. A Sovereign Citizen. That agrees to work for the good of the whole, not just a few -"

At that moment Con Poulos came barrelling into the Main Bar area, startling some of the people watching the television. He saw Alexia at the bar and rushed up to her.

"Quick change it to Channel 8," he yelled.

Midst cat calls for Con to sit down and be quiet, Alexia Aristis gave him a horrible stare. "They're talking about the town Con, so sit down and shut up."

"But on Channel 4 the Opposition Leader is here," he protested.

"Shut up! This is bullshit," yelled Koz.

"What?" said Alexia Aristis.

"Channel 8 is broadcasting outside right this minute!" yelled Con Poulos.

Alexia presses the remote control to howls and abuse from the bar.

"Everyone shut up," she growled.

The television now revealed the image of Ken Bright speaking to the Opposition Leader in front of the Eelang Arms Hotel with the TV graphic Live From Eelang.

"Now we are all on telly!" yelled Koz.

"So what do you hope to achieve here in Eelang Opposition Leader?" asked Ken Bright on the television broadcast.

****

Koz was the first to step outside the bar and see what was going on. The lights of the live broadcast made the front of the hotel like daylight, as the rest of the locals poured out of the bar to also have a look.

"Well, Ken," smiled Peter Vicar, "I hope to speak with some of the locals of Eelang and maybe even Percy Hamilton -"

"King Percy," interrupted Ken Bright.

"Right. King Percy, and let them know that all of Australia is behind them as I am against these greedy banks and the government taking away the homes and businesses of hard working people."

Applause from the crowd now watching the filming from outside the Hotel.

"Well Opposition Leader, it looks like the people of Eelang like what you are saying," smiled Ken Bright. "Maybe, we can get a couple of them over right now and you can say it to them directly?"

Peter Vicar at first visibly tensed up as Ken Bright left his chair off camera, before Peter Vicar smiled cautiously at the camera and then glanced at the vacant seats next to him.

"Yes, I'd like to speak to a couple of people from Eelang," he smiled feebly.

"Kingdom of Eelang," yelled Koz from off camera.

"Right. Kingdom of Eelang," replied Peter Vicar.

****

The Prime Minister strode along a corridor of the ministerial wing of Parliament House as Marion Alright scurried up to him.

"Ah Marion, I thought we did rather well in diffusing that little chestnut."

Marion is frowning.

"We have another problem."

The Prime Minister looked puzzled as Marion opened the door to an office with the writing PRIME MINISTER on the door.

The Prime Minister entered the office and turned to see the television tuned to Channel 8 and Ken Bright from *This Day Tonight* with a nervous looking Koz sitting on the centre chair with Peter Vicar still in his chair with the graphics *Live From Eelang* at the bottom of the screen.

"Shit," said the Prime Minister.

****

Ken Bright signalled to Koz as the live broadcast continued.

"So Mr Koz is that your full name or a nick name? And what is it you do for a living?"

"Am I on telly now?"

Ken Bright smiled condescendingly. "Yes Mr Koz you are live on television to millions of Australians."

Wonderment and nerves wash across the face of Koz.

"My, my name is Leonid Kozlovarenchenko. But people call me Koz."

"Right. Thank goodness," said Ken Bright.

"I, I am a mechanic. A car mechanic. I am self employed."

Koz then spontaneously turned to Peter Vicar and extended both his hands, as Peter Vicar nervously extended his hand and Koz started to shake his hand vigorously. "Thank you Mr Prime Minister for coming to help us."

Ken Bright laughed.

"Ah Mr Koz, Mr Vicar is not the Prime Minister...yet"

****

The Prime Minister put his hand to his head. "Shit. And Double shit."

The Prime Minister swung around to Marion Alright. "Get me to Eelang now!"

Marion Alright scurried away.

******

At the Channel 8 studios, Angela Kostakos and her producer (Warren) were also watching the broadcast of Channel 4 from a monitor on the set. Both shook their heads.

"And what would you like to say personally to the banks tonight Mr Koz?"

Koz looked straight at the camera and leant forward with his fiercest face. "I say to banks what you do to us is wrong. It is bullshit!"

Ken Bright erupted in a fake half hearted laugh.

"I understand your frustration. I just hope the desk caught that before it went to air."

"What? I cannot say bullshit in my own country? What is wrong with the word bullshit?"

Angela Kostakos turned off the Monitor and looked at Warren. "They scooped us Warren," she growled. "No one does that to me and gets away with it."

******

Ed Cartwright and Lewis Botta were sitting nervously in their hotel room upstairs at the Eelang Arms Hotel when there was a firm knock at the door. Both men jumped with fright. Ed Cartwright looked at Lewis who then shook his head and pointed back at Ed Cartwright.

Another knock, this time louder and more insistent. Ed Cartwright firmly pointed his finger at Lewis Botta who huffed and got up from his chair and tip-toed over to the door and peered through the peep hole. Outside the room door was a shorter man (Victor) in clean dark grey overalls, carrying a case and looking very impatient. Victor now started to bang harder on the door.

With a look of horror on the face of Lewis Botta, he turned around to Ed Cartwright and mouthed the words, "The Cleaner."

Fed up, Ed Cartwright got up from his chair and nudged Lewis Botta out of the way. At first Lewis tried to obstruct him from opening the door by applying the latch lock.

Ed Cartwright opened the door and it was stopped by the latch. Ed Cartwright squeezed his face through the gap and smiled meekly at Victor. He could now see that Victor was in fact carrying two large bags.

"Yes? Can I help you?"

"I am the cleaner," said Victor in a heavy Russian accent.

Ed Cartwright looked nervous.

"I am Victor," repeated Victor.

A clear yelp from Lewis Botta obscured by the door.

"You have dog in room? Dog no good. I am allergic to dog."

Ed Cartwright nodded negatively as he became bright red from a look of fear and adrenalin.

"You let me in now or I call Mr Fay."

Ed Cartwright shook his head negatively and closed the door, before the fumbling of the chain being taken off and some kind of brief scuffle. The door opened fully this time and Victor stepped into the room with his cases.

Inside the room, Victor did not waste any time. He put his first bag on a table and opens it, producing a hand full of micro cameras. Ed Cartwright and Lewis Botta both exhale a sigh of relief, as Victor looks at both of them strangely.

Next, Victor produced what looks like a gun and both men step back, before Victor produces a second part being a listening dish and attached the two pieces together.

"Now we set bugs and cameras and then watch and listen, no?"

****

Ed Cartwright and Lewis Botta were sitting impatiently in the front of a blue van. Across the road was Kate's House.

"Why does he need us to do this with him?" asked Lewis Botta.

Ed Cartwright shrugged his shoulders.

"I hope he hurries up. I need to pee," complained Lewis Botta.

Awkward silence.

"Do you think he has killed people?" asked Lewis Botta.

"Who?"

"The Cleaner. Victor."

Ed Cartwright smiled. "We are a bank aren't we?"

At that moment, the driver's door swung open and both Lewis Botta and Ed Cartwright jump.Victor got into the van shaking his head, before sneezing. "He has dog. I hate dog."

He sneezed again before they drove off.

Chapter 6

A new spirit was in the air of the town as Percy and Kate were standing with their eyes closed next to Harry Feldon in front of his shop.

"OK, now open your eyes," said Harry Feldon.

Both Percy and Kate opened their eyes and looked at the front of the shop with a new banner saying *Eelang Royal News And Souvenirs* and start nodding their heads.

"It's lovely," smiled Kate politely.

"It's great isn't it?" smiled Harry Feldon

Harry Feldon ran off into his shop as Percy and Kate looked at each other before Harry returned with an armful of items. He handed a plate to Percy, with a picture of Percy and the writing Kingdom Of Eelang on it.

"See Percy, we have Royal Plates, and Royal Mugs."

Harry handed the mug of Kingdom Of Eelang to Kate.

"We have Royal Tea Towels," he said enthusiastically. "And next week we will even have Royal Stamps and Commemorative Coins."

Percy looked at Kate again and shrugged his shoulders.

****

A new morning in Eelang and the whole town is out in the main street, preparing flags and bunting. A stage is being prepared in the centre of the road, with the banner *Kingdom of Eelang Welcomes Australian PM*.

The television host Ken Bright and his camera crew were walking along the street, filming the transformation. "Hello this is Ken Bright from *This Day Tonight* on Channel 8 reporting to you live from Eelang that is a town in a frenzy, as the Prime Ministers' Office announced that he will be coming tomorrow to make a special policy announcement at midday."

****

Sophie and Ben Lang struggled to give Rex a bath, with Rex looking less than impressed.

****

Koz presented Percy his Mercedes with a new coat of paint and cleaned up like new, to the applause of the crowd.

****

Percy, Kate and Rex were sitting on the grassy Headland watching the sunset. Percy reached over to hold the hand of Kate as she smiles at him.

"I can't believe how you did it. But the town has never been more united."

"It was your brother Jack who gave me the idea. Anyway, I am sorry for all the strife I have caused you and the kids."

Percy moved a little closer.

"I just don't want Ben or Sophie to get hurt again, or the town," smiled Percy. "And I don't want to hurt you anymore Miss Kate Lang."

Percy reached over and kissed Kate passionately. Kate pulled back for a moment, slightly stunned, before they kissed again.

"I love you miss Kate."

"I know. It just took you ten years to finally admit it."

****

Inside the CEO's Office of OmniBank, Ellis Pickering was sitting, while Martin Fay was pacing around. Marion Alright, the Chief Of Staff of the Prime Minister was near the door to the office watching Martin Fay as he circled around like some caged animal.

"So nothing. You've found nothing," said Martin Fay.

"That is correct," said Victor on the phone in reply.

Inside Ed Cartwrights room, Victor, Ed Cartwright and Lewis Botta were huddled around a phone on speaker, surrounded by monitoring equipment and video feeds from multiple bugs.

"No drugs, no guns, no gambling," said Victor. "These are the most boring people I have ever seen."

"But the food is nice and fresh," added Lewis Botta.

Both Ed Cartwright and Victor stare at Lewis Botta who shrugged his shoulders.

"Anything you find," barked Martin Fay. "Anything, you call me immediately."

Martin Fay pressed the button on the speaker phone and ended the call.

"You sure there is nothing you can do to stall your boss?" asked Martin Fay to Marion Alright.

Marion Alright shook her head negatively. "I am on your side. But you created this mess, remember?"

"What about that judge of ours on the foreclosure case?" asked Ellis Pickering to Martin Fay.

"Justice O'Rourke," replied Martin Fay. "It's already happening but won't stop the media tomorrow."

Marion Alright put her hands to her ears and started walking toward the door.

"Gentlemen, I don't want to know your dirty little secrets," she said.

Marion Alright opened the door to the CEO's office to leave.

"So unless you can come up with some kind of miracle by tomorrow there is nothing I can do."

Marion Alright left the office. Ellis Pickering signals to Martin Fay.

"You go with her to Eelang and see if there is some way of forestalling this train wreck?"

Martin Fay nodded and chased after Marion Alright.

King and Country

Chapter 7

A television van with the slogan *Boiling Point* emblazoned across it, arrived into Eelang. It stopped and parked in front of the Eelang General Store, beside another television van with the logo *This Day Tonight* all across it.

Angela Kostakos got out of the Boiling Point television van with her crew Warren and Mazza. They walked up to the *This Day Tonight* television van in front, leant down and jammed a match stick into the air valve of the back left wheel, causing a hissing sound as the air started to escape. Angela Kostakos smiled, before she looked at the window of the General Store and stepped in.

Inside, Vivien Li was at the front counter of the General Store. She smiled politely at Angela Kostakos as the TV host and her camera crew entered. Angela Kostakos turned down the vegetable and fruit aisle and walked straight into Ken Bright, Susie Radcliff and her television crew.

"You!" yelled Angela Kostakos.

Ken Bright smiled condescendingly and turned to Susie Radcliff.

"Look Susie," he said, "its yesterdays news."

There were chuckles from the Channel 4 crew as a furious Angela Kostakos picked up a tomato and threw it at the head of Ken Bright. Instinctively, Ken put up his arm and the tomato deflected and hit Susie Radcliff in the face. Now the chuckles came from the Channel 8 crew.

"You bitch!" yelled Susie Radcliff at Angela Kostakos. "You've had it now. I know karate."

Susie Radcliff then adopted a classic karate position, before moving against Angela Kostakos. But instead of backing off, Angela Kostakos herself assumed a martial arts position and matched the attack moves of Susie Radcliff.

Frustrated, Susie Radcliff grabbed various vegetables and threw them at Angela Kostakos. Yet Angela Kostakos proved herself an equally skilled adversary as the men watched on in awe.

"Ten years Showlin hard core training baby," growled Angela Kostakos. "So bring it on!"

Angela Kostakos motioned for Susie Radcliff to bring it on, before Susie Radcliff grabbed a broom and snapped it into two fighting sticks. Angela Kostakos did the same, by grabbing two toilet plungers and stripping off the rubber ends. The TV journalists continued to duel it out as the men continued to watch on.

But just as Angela Kostakos was getting the upper hand against Susie Radcliff and looked like she could inflict some serious damage, out of no where came the store owner Vivian Li. She stepped in and within seconds foot swept Angela Kostakos as well as Susie Radcliff onto the ground.

"No one does karate in my store except me," screamed Vivien Li.

The television journalists looked stunned at the exhibition of martial arts of Vivien Li that floored them Angela and Susie in the blink of an eye. Vivien Li then looked around at the mess.

"You clean up mess," barked Vivien Li. "You pay and then you give me good television interview or I karate all of you!"

The television crew all nodded nervously and started to help clean up the mess.

****

Percy was about to step into his caravan when Rex stopped. Percy looked over at Rex who focused on the Caravan.

"What is it Rex?"

Percy looked to the side of the caravan and a baseball bat that was lying next to some fence posts. He grabbed the bat and swung open the door to reveal what looked like a homeless man with a bag (Barry Bruce) sitting inside.

"No Percy, its me!" grinned Barry Bruce.

Percy looked at this figure strangely, until Barry Bruce started to pull off his disguise.

"Its me, Barry Bruce."

****

Lewis Botta was sitting in front of the television monitors, falling asleep as Victor walked over and looked at the monitor of the camera in Percys Caravan. He hit Lewis over the side of the head.

"Ow!"

"Caravan," said Victor. "Look. Someone with Percy."

Lewis Botta shook himself up and enlarged up the monitor screen image showing Percy inside the Caravan with Barry Bruce.

"Barry, the whole town and federal police are looking for you," said Percy.

"I know and I am sorry I left in such a hurry and did not explain myself," replied Barry Bruce. "But that was before I saw what you were doing."

Victor looked at Lewis Botta.

"You have Recording on? yes?"

Lewis Botta nodded affirmatively.

"Good. Very good," smiled Victor.

****

Inside Percy's Caravan, Barry Bruce opened the bag in front of him and then pushed it to Percy, who looked inside before pulling out a large wad of 100 dollar notes.

"What is this?"

"This is the money...well a lot of it..a fair bit of it from the development deal. "

Percy looked a little perplexed. "Your plan of declaring yourself sovereign and declaring Eelang a Kingdom is pure bloody genius!" exclaimed Barry Bruce. "What with the merchandising and tourism alone, we could have a bag like this every month!"

Percy shook his head in disgust. "Don't give me that," he growled at Barry Bruce. "You knew what we were doing when we did the deal with OmniBank and you know exactly what you are doing with this whole King and Country show."

Percy zipped up the bag and pushed it back at Barry Bruce.

"I was only doing it with you because I thought it would help the town. I don't give a damn about tea towels or commemorative coins or flags. I just want to save the town that is my home," said Percy.

Barry Bruce started laughing. "Seriously. You'd throw this whole opportunity away?"

"Barry you need to leave," said Percy.

Barry Bruce shook his head.

"I was only joking Percy, lighten up."

"Barry, you are a wanted fugitive. You need to leave now and don't come back here ever again, or anywhere around Kate or her kids, or so help me I will do what the rest of the town wants to happen to you. Now GET OUT!"

Barry looked stunned at first, before picking up his bag and leaving Percy in his caravan alone with Rex.

Chapter 8

The main street of Eelang was a throng of people waiting for the arrival of the Prime Minister and his announcement.

On the stage in the middle of the main street, Percy was standing with Kate, Harry Feldon, Koz, Vivian Li and Mary-Ann McNamara as people were milling around. Harry Feldon moved forward to a lectern, almost obscured by media microphones as Kate looked over at Percy who seemed lost in thought.

"Check One, Two," spluttered Harry Feldon. "Ooonnneee, Twwwooo."

Kate looked at Percy.

"What's on your mind?" she asked. "You're somewhere else at the moment."

Percy gave a half smile. "I'll tell you later."

"Ladies and Gentlemen," said Harry Feldon over the p.a. system. "The Prime Minister should be here any moment now."

****

Behind the Podium Marion Alright was standing with Ed Cartwright and Martin Fay. Ed Cartwright was holding a two-way radio to his ear and a small portable video monitor in his other hand. Ed Cartwright looked up at a nearby lamp post.

"Are you seeing us and hearing this Victor?"

****

In the Eelang arms hotel, Victor was sitting at the control desk studying the monitors with Lewis Botta. As they watch one of the monitors shows the figures of Marion Alright with Martin Fay and Ed Cartwright.

"I got it," replied Victor into a two way radio.

"They're ready to see the footage, can you play it now?"

"OK, playing now," added Victor.

****

On the Main Street behind the podium, Ed Cartwright held up the monitor for Marion Alright and Martin Fay to see while they each plug in an ear piece to hear. The video feed started.

"Wow," said Martin Fay.

"Excellent," said Marion Alright.

The video feed stopped and Ed Cartwright threw a thumbs up at the hidden camera on top of the lamp post.

"Can your boys have the edited video ready for an exclusive in the next hour?" asked Marion Alright.

Martin Fay looked at Ed Cartwright who nodded affirmatively.

"Good. No one is to breathe a word of this," said Marion Alright. "The Prime Minister is on his way. If you agree with your promise to get the big banks to voluntarily cut half a percentage in interest rates on cue after his hard hitting anti-bank speech, then I can have a couple of the agents already here make the move and get him back to the city."

"Sure. A deal is a deal," smiled Martin Fay. "Take Barry Bruce by all means, but why not keep Percy local for a couple of days before sending him to the city? All the gravitas to fully sink in while the media is in town."

Marion shrugged her shoulders before she moved away.

"It is up to you. Whatever," she said. "But you have only a few minutes, because I am calling the PM now."

Marion pulled out her phone and walks away.

****

Percy and Kate were standing on the stage when Martin Fay walked up onto the stage accompanied by two suited federal police officers.

"Who are you?" asked Kate.

"Martin Fay, Legal Counsel, Omnibank."

"If you've come to confess. Too late. Otherwise get off our stage!" she yelled.

Martin Fay signalled to the two federal officers, who then surrounded Percy.

40

"Actually Miss Lang, I have come to witness your confession," grinned Martin Fay, "or the town to be more precise."

The crowd gasped as they witness the event.

"Percy Hamilton, you are under arrest," said the first federal officer, "for suspicion of cheating and defraud."

Percy shook his head negatively. "I don't understand?"

The handcuffs were now on Percy as he was escorted off the stage to the howls of the crowd. Martin Fay moved to the microphone and produced a piece of paper.

"Now, now. I know this is all very dramatic," smiled Martin Fay to the crowd. "But let me explain."

Marion Alright signalled to the Federal Officers who then handed Percy to Sgt Jagamara.

Martin Fay briefly glanced down at the proceedings and smiled before continuing.

"Unfortunately the circus has to come to an end," said Martin Fay, "for the reason of law and justice to prevail."

Boos from the crowd.

"Yes you can boo all you like," added Martin Fay. "You can wish and protest all you like, but I have here a signed order from the Supreme Court that in two days will decide on the order to hand over all of Eelang to Omnibank."

Now there were hurls of abuse and angry shouts. Martin Fay looked down again.

Sgt Jagamara made sure Percy didn't bump his head while he was placed in the back of the Police car. Sgt. Jagamara walked around to the drivers side and got in.

Martin Fay shook his head to the crowd.

"Don't blame the bank. Blame Percy! He is the one that deceived you and told you lies! Now the bank has no choice but to protect its reputation and bring this entire side show to an end."

****

At the Eelang Police Station, Sgt. Jagamara took off the handcuffs before closing the steel bar door with Percy in the cell.

"Jagamara, I didn't cheat or defraud the town."

Sgt. Jagamara shrugged his shoulders.

"But you sure pissed them off Percy. And whatever they have on you, it must be top shelf, otherwise they wouldn't be wanting to roast you slowly."

Percy sat down on the cell bed and put his head in his hands.

Chapter 9

The TV vans were all parked at the Eelang Arms Hotel. The Main Bar of the hotel was full of journalists and outsiders, who had come to watch the spectacle. People were swapping stories and discussing the events of the day. Even Ed Cartwright, Victor and Lewis Botta were drinking in celebration. Just a couple of locals (Con Poulos and Bertrone Camilleri) were there, looking sombre and distraught.

Angela Kostakos with her team of Warren and Mazza were sitting at a table drinking, while Susie Radcliff and her team were sitting at a table further away, smiling and animated. When Susie locks eyes on Angela, she raised her glass and Angela Kostakos nods politely.

"What are they so chipper about?" asked Angela Kostakos.

"Everyone shut up," yelled Alexia Aristis. "There is something breaking on the telly."

The bar shuts up and look up at the television set to see a beaming Ken Bright with the banner Breaking Exclusive News and Live From Eelang.

"Hello Australia, this is Ken Bright, host of This Day Tonight sharing with you a breaking exclusive on the story that has shocked us all with the arrest of Percy Hamilton, or King Percy as he has called himself. Channel 8 has obtained exclusive footage that proves Percy Hamilton is nothing more than a criminal mastermind that sought to trick the good people of Eelang and the Australian public."

"What the?" stuttered Angela Kostakos.

Mumbling around the bar as Susie Radcliff is beaming.

"Everyone shut up," yelled Alexia Aristis.

The Bar shuts up again as the television and audio taken from inside Percy's Caravan was shown on television, from the moment Barry Bruce opens the bag in front of him and then pushes it to Percy, who looked inside before pulling out a large wad of 100 dollar notes.

"What is this?" asked Percy from the tape on television.

"This is the money," replies Barry Bruce in the edited tape. "Well a lot of it from the development deal. Your plan of declaring yourself sovereign and declaring Eelang a Kingdom is pure bloody genius! What with the merchandising and tourism alone, we could have a bag like this every month! You knew what we were doing when we did the deal with OmniBank and you know exactly what you are doing with this whole King and Country show."

The clip ended with Percy zipping up the bag, before returning to a head shot of Ken Bright shaking his head.

"Those double crossing snake shits -" grumbled Angela Kostakos as she stared at the opposing television crew.

"A sad day for Eelang," said Ken Bright on the television. "And a sad day for all of Australia that trusted Percy Hamilton."

Angela Kostakos looked over at Susie Radcliff who raised her glass to her.

"Someone gave that moron the footage," said Angela Kostakos to Warren and Mozza sitting with her. "And they are probably still here celebrating."

Angela Kostakos scanned around the bar and back to Ed Cartwright in a suit, Victor and Lewis Botta all drinking and celebrating. She narrowed her gaze.

****

Kate was crying when she heard a knock at the door. She opened it to see Bart Manning sober.

"My dear," smiled Bart. "I know you have only known me as an annoying drunk of the town. But I come to you completely sober. Let me re-introduce myself. I am Bart Manning QC and if you let me help you I firmly am of the opinion that we can beat this bloody bank."

Kate started crying and gave him a hug.

****

It was late at night at the Eelang Arms Hotel and the carpark outside was almost empty.

Inside, the Main Bar has cleared out of most people, except for Angela Kostakos, a few locals and Ed Cartwright, Victor and Lewis Botta.

"I feel sick," said Ed Cartwright. "I am going to bed."

Ed Cartwright gets up and staggers to the door. Victor looks at Lewis Botta who is still trying to drink his drink and then Victor gets up himself.

"Goodnight," said Victor to Lewis Botta. "I pack up and leave in morning."

Lewis Botta tried to signal OK, but was too drunk to complete the salute. Once Victor left, Angela Kostakos came over to the table of Lewis Botta.

"Do you mind if I join you?" smiled Angela Kostakos.

Lewis steadied himself. "Sure. I am not with him," he slurred.

Lewis pointed to an empty chair before realizing his mistake. Lewis then focuses on her more closely.

"You are pretty up close. Not as scary as the Angela Kontansa on television."

Angela Kostakos laughs and smiled. "Kostakos," she corrected him. "But you have the advantage as I do not yet know your name?

Lewis extends his hand. "Lewis. Lewis Botta."

"What an incredible day?" she asked. "Eh Lewis?"

Lewis Botta nodded. "The greatest. The greatest of my life and a huge promotion."

"Really? Well Lewis, I suppose your footage of Percy Hamilton sealed it then."

Lewis Botta nodded again and then puts his finger to his mouth. "Shhh. It is a secret."

"Absolutely yes we must keep it a secret. I just wanted to see it one more time for myself. You know? Just to remember and celebrate?"

"Marion told us to keep it under wraps. Shhh."

"Oh you mean Marion Alright?"

Lewis Botta nodded as his eyes roll in his head.

"Marion and I are old friends. I am sure she wouldn't mind as we will keep it a secret. So where have you kept all the tapes for Marion?"

Lewis pointed upstairs. Angela got up from her chair and started to lift Lewis Botta out of his as he is fading fast.

"Best we get you upstairs then to bed, don't you think?"

Lewis nodded again and puts his finger to his lips.

Angela Kostakos dragged the half asleep and very drunk Lewis Botta up the stairs and down the hallway to the door.

"This one?"

Lewis Botta nods and then completely passes out. Angela then ruffles through his pockets and finds the key and let her self in. Next, she dragged Lewis into the room by his legs.

Inside the room, Ed Cartwright was already in bed snoring as Angela Kostakos finishes dragging Lewis into the room and then tip-toes over to the monitors and control desk that have all been turned off. She presses the on button and then freezes as Ed Cartwright stops snoring and turns over, before realizing he is still completely out of it.

Angela Kostakos then re-wound the recording to find the taped meeting of Marion Alright and Martin Fay behind the podium. She plugs in an ear piece and starts smiling ear to ear.

"Jackpot!" she whispered.

Chapter 10

In the police station cells, Percy was crawled up in a foetal position under a blanket, trying to sleep.

There was a tap on the cell bars. Percy rolled over slowly to see it was Fr Jack.

"Come to give me last rights Fr Jack?"

"Let's just say Percy that if I was not a man of God and willing to forgive, I could think of worse things."

"I suppose it doesn't really help much if I were to tell you that I didn't do what they claimed," said Percy. "They chopped the tape to suit their ends."

"Anyway Percy I've come to let you know that Kate and the kids have moved your Caravan out to Headland Park. But Rex is fine and the kids are taking good care of him."

Percy nodded his head. "Thanks for letting me know."

Through the windows, bright lights were flickering as chants increase from outside.

Sgt. Jagamara, who was watching television, got up from his chair. "Shit I hope it is not what I think it is?" he said as he walked to the window.

Sgt. Jagamara turned around to Fr Jack. "Stay put Fr. Jack. I think some white fellas are stirring up some trouble out the front of my station."

Sgt. Jagamara put on his hat and stepped outside.

Outside, a crowd carrying signs HANG PERCY and JUSTICE NOW FOR EELANG were at the front of the police station. Several cars, had their lights aimed at the station.

"What is going on here?" said Sgt. Jagamara.

"Hang Percy. Hang Percy," yelled the crowd of locals.

Sgt. Jagamara waved his hands.

"Settle down. Settle down. There will be no riots against white fellas in prison on my watch. So best you be getting back to your homes before I have to start shooting you people."

47

****

Inside the police station, Fr Jack and Percy continued to speak.

"I never meant for any of this to happen Jack, especially not Kate."

"I know you are good man Percy. But honestly you've got to grow up at some stage and see that the old road to that other place is paved with all your good intentions."

"Please tell your sister Kate I am sorry and I truly do love her, no matter what she thinks of me," said Percy.

"Kate is going to the city with Bart Manning tomorrow to stop this foreclosure case."

"Bart Manning, the drunk Bart Manning?" asked Percy.

"Not anymore," smiled Fr. Jack. "He has gone cold turkey and stark cold sober."

Percy shook his head.

"So if there is hope for Bart Manning," said Fr. Jack, "then maybe there is hope even for you Percy Hamilton?"

Chapter 11

A classic metropolitan courthouse building. Inside, Bart Manning was in his best barristers outfit with Kate sitting next to him, looking nervous. On the other side is the Plaintiff Counsel (Wade Pemberton), looking suitably smug. He caught the eye of Bart Manning and smirked.

"Don't be nervous," smiled Bart Manning to Kate. "It is all theatre and bluster. It is supposed to intimidate you. But really it nothing more than Pirates of the Penzance."

"What is Pirates of Penzanze?" whispered Kate.

A man entered the court carrying a rod. "All Rise," he shouted.

"19th Century hocus pocus. Gilbert and Sullivan were the Andrew Lloyd Weber of their day," added Bart Manning.

The courtroom stood up as the judge entered and ceremonially bowed.

"The Supreme Court is now in Session," yelled the man with the black rod. "The Honorable Mr Justice Edward O'Rourke Presiding."

The judge gave Bart Manning a foul look. "Now Counsel for the Defence, what is this motion I see before me for seeking an apprehended bias order? I will not be granting such orders."

"Then your Honour having read it, fully agrees with its premise," replied Bart Manning calmly.

"No. No I do not agree with its contents," grumbled the judge. "Don't play games with me counsel."

"Very well, is it the wish of your honour to hear the matter fairly and impartially?"

"Yes of course," said the judge condescendingly.

"And your honour gives his word on oath on that?"

"I am a judge aren't I? Yes and you are pushing it."

"Very well, I seek leave of your honour to withdraw the said motion, if your honour may answer one final question, seeing as though you have agreed under oath to act fairly and impartially, can you then assure the court you have no pecuniary interest in this matter?"

"Right, I've had enough of you, you little shit - " yelled the judge.

Bart Manning nodded as Justice O'Rourke got up from the bench and huffed off, before the court got up. Wade Pemberton, the Plaintiff Counsel for the Bank looked dumbfounded at what just happened.

"What just happened?" asked Kate.

"When a judge accepts to hear a case, he naturally has to take a fiduciary interest," replied Bart Manning. "Thus, if he gives an oath to act in his judicial capacity, to be free and impartial, then he cannot possibly continue. A chess piece has been removed from the board. One step closer my dear."

****

It was mid morning and Ed Cartwright and Lewis Botta were still in bed, when there is a loud knocking at the door, followed by insistent thumping.

"Go away," groaned Ed Cartwright.

"Open the bloody door Cartwright," yelled Martin Fay.

Martin Fay stood in the hallway with Victor out the front of the room, bashing on the door again.

Ed Cartwright got up slowly as Lewis Botta remains spread out like a starfish and passed out on his bed. As soon as he opens the door, Martin Fay and Victor barrelled past him to the machinery, almost pushing him over.

"Hey," stuttered Ed Cartwright.

Victor was the first to look and turned to Martin Fay, shaking his head negatively.

"It was definitely all turned off and several DAT tapes are missing."

"Shit, Shit, Shit," said Martin Fay.

Martin Fay stomped over to Ed Cartwright who was in the midst of trying to pour a glass of water. Martin Fay snatched it off of him, slammed it down on the table and then grabbed Ed Cartwright.

"Now think very hard Cartwright," said Martin Fay menacingly. "After you went to your room last night, what did you and your buddy do?"

Ed Cartwright shrugged his shoulders.

"I went to bed. What is all the stress about?"

"Because Angela Kostakos on Channel 4 is running an exclusive on the extended footage that drops a pile of elephant dung on Ken Bright and the PM and us."

"Oh," said Ed Cartwright. "Oh shit."

"If that is your best answer then you can tell Pickering yourself as your coming back to the city with me."

"What about me?" asked Lewis Botta as he opened his eyes.

"I haven't decided what to do with you yet. For the moment you will do whatever Victor wants you to do and pack all this up now."

Lewis Botta nodded nervously as Victor stepped up and started to dismantle the equipment.

****

Kate and Bart Manning were back in the court, with Wade Pemberton looking far less confident. The Black Rod arrived calling all rise.

"I know Jim," whispered Bart Manning. "He is a good judge."

Judge (Justice (James) Peters) walked in and sat down before he looked over at Bart Manning and Kate with a smile and then a frown.

"No stunts counsel?"

"No stunts your honour," bowed Bart Manning.

"Very well," said the judge, "I call the Counsel for the Plaintiff to make their opening remarks."

Wade Pemberton got up and bowed to the judge.

"Thank you, your honour. I'd like to begin by reminding the court of the illustrious foundation of the Bank and its part in shaping the affairs of this state and nation."

Bart Manning rolled his eyes as Justice Peters tried to maintain the appearance of interest.

****

For what seemed like an eternity, Wade Pemberton continued speaking and speaking, with exhibit after exhibit. Bart Manning and the judge and the rest of the court struggled to stay awake. Finally Pemberton finished.

"And that concludes the opening arguments for the bank your honour," said Wade Pemberton.

"Very well," said the judge. "Does the defence wish to commence their opening remarks or shall we adjourn until tomorrow?"

Bart Manning shook his head. As he got up, he rubbed his arm and Kate reached out, before Bart Manning smiled and signalled he was fine.

"No thank you your honour. I won't need nearly as much time to outline the arguments of the defence. Just a few minutes."

Justice Peters nodded. "Proceed."

Bart Manning, turned to Wade Pemberton. "I have but three questions I wish to address to the learned counsel on my left."

Wade Pemberton looked at Justice Peters and then back at Bart Manning and then back at the judge who shrugged his shoulder.

"I object. This is irrelevant," complained Wade Pemberton.

"For the benefit of the court, I remind my psychic colleague I haven't asked the questions yet."

Justice Peters chuckled.

"Objection denied. I strongly urge counsel to ensure the questions are appropriate. You promised no stunts."

Bart Manning smiled and then looks back at Wade Pemberton who now stood up.

"My first question to my learned colleague is, that given it is an irrefutable fact that the surveyed and posted land of Eelang was first granted effectively under Royal Patent in 1820: show me then the law that circumvents such title?"

"The Australian Constitution," said Wade Pemberton proudly.

"Never ratified by any state. Not one Statute of ratification on the books for any state. Alas an English statute being nothing more than a Patent itself with a few corporate by-laws - "

"But, but this is a court of Australia and the state of -"

"If I may, my second question?" interrupted Bart Manning.

Wade looked desperately at the judge who then nodded at Bart Manning to proceed.

"My second question then to my most learned colleague is, that given the Royal Land Patent granted to Charles Edward Lang preceded the patent and charter granted to forming the state, by what title is our learned colleague claiming merit and therefore his claim of right?"

"State lands and titles," said Wade Pemberton, less confidently.

"Ah. So despite the fact it is an inferior land claim, you know and I know and the court knows that there hasn't been proper land title recordings for more then twenty-five years. Besides, all the states are corporations now as well -"

"Your honour please -" cried Wade Pemberton.

Justice Peters smiled.

"I think he has one more question," said the judge.

Bart Manning bowed and returns to squaring off against Wade Pemberton.

"So my final question to my erudite and most lucid colleague is, that given any claim of injury or default or delinquency must first show a meeting of the minds, by what form of law is our colleague claiming such tort?"

"You know the answer," grinned Wade Pemberton. "It is Contract law."

"Ah contract, yes. But false, deceptive and misleading acts, otherwise known as fraud negates any such contract, especially one done in bad faith does it not?"

Your honour.

"The court shall adjourn till tomorrow morning."

The court rose but as Kate and Bart Manning were leaving, Bart Manning stumbled and then collapsed. Kate dropped down next to him as Bart is holding his arm.

"Bart? Bart are you OK?" she asked frantically.

Kate looked up as the Bailiff and court attendants as they rush over.

"Will someone please get a doctor," she yelled.

King and Country

Chapter 12

The OmniBank building at night. Inside the CEO's Office, Ellis Pickering was sitting, while Martin Fay and Ed Cartwright were standing.

"Double, do you understand? We will double your payment if you find or get rid of any evidence of that land patent," said Ellis Pickering.

At the other end of the phone, Victor and Lewis Botta were sitting in the van at night watching from across the road the light spectacle of a television broadcast out the front of the Eelang Arms Hotel.

"Find the land patent," yelled Ellis Pickering and hung up the phone.

****

Victor put his phone down and looked at Lewis Botta.

"So what now?" asked Lewis Botta.

"Now we go find this document."

Victor started up the van.

****

Ellis Pickering narrowed his gaze at Ed Cartwright as Martin Fay pressed the remote on the television to reveal a picture of Angela Kostakos from Boiling Point with the graphic *Exclusive Breaking News Live* From Eelang.

"You have really screwed us Cartwright," mumbled Martin Fay.

Cartwright shook his head as Martin Fay turned up the volume on the television.

"I can explain," he spluttered.

"It'll have to wait," snapped Martin Fay. "The show is about to start."

On television was the image of a serious faced Angela Kostakos standing outside the Eelang Arms Hotel.

"*Good evening Australia, I am Angela Kostakos from Boiling Point. Tonight we are broadcasting to you live from Eelang with a reporter standing by at Omnibank Headquarters.*"

The television program cut to another female reporter (Ellie Marshall) standing outside the front of the Omnibank Headquarters.

"And a reporter in Canberra."

The television program cut to a television reporter standing in front of a security guard at Parliament House in Canberra.

"Tonight, Boiling Point will be revealing to the Australian people a shocking conspiracy between the Office of the Prime Minister and Omnibank against the people of Eelang and Percy Hamilton."

"Shit," said Martin Fay.

Angela Kostakos continued on her opening monologue.

"We begin with footage we have handed to the Federal Police proving the conspiracy."

The footage taken from the monitoring equipment of Ed Cartwright, Martin Fay and Marion Alright behind the podium at Eelang was now broadcast on the television program, including the audio from the secret meeting.

"Can your boys have the edited video ready for an exclusive in the next hour?"

On television, Martin Fay looked at Ed Cartwright who nodded affirmatively.

"Good," said Marion Alright on the broadcast footage. *"No one is to breathe a word of this. The Prime Minister is on his way. If you agree with your promise to get the big banks to voluntarily cut half a percent in interest rates on cue after his hard hitting anti-bank speech, then I can have a couple of the agents already here make the move and get him back to the city..."*

As the footage on the television continued in the background, there was a loud knock at the door of the CEO's office.

"Not now, for God's sake!" yelled Ellis Pickering.

The door opened anyway to reveal two federal Police Officers who stepped inside the Office and over to Martin Fay and Ed Cartwright.

"Martin Fay, Ed Cartwright Federal Police. You are both under arrest on suspicion for conspiracy."

The first Federal Officer handcuffed Martin Fay.

"Shit," said Martin Fay.

The two Federal Officers then escorted Martin Fay and Ed Cartwright out of the office in handcuffs.

****

In front of the Omnibank headquarters was the reporter Ellie Marshall and her camera crew live. As soon as they saw Martin Fay in handcuffs, they ran over to confront him.

"That's right Angela," said Ellie Marshall, "we are just seeing Exclusive footage of Police arresting Omnibank officials regarding this shocking conspiracy."

Ellie then shoved a microphone in the face of Martin Fay as he was being escorted to a waiting unmarked police car.

"Mr Fay, Mr Fay, what do you have to say to the Australian public and the people of Eelang?" she demanded.

"Get that thing out of my face," growled Martin Fay.

The police put Ed Cartwright into the car, followed by Martin Fay.

"Mr Fay, what do you want to say to Omnibank shareholders?"

Martin Fay snarled back at Ellie Marshall. "You can all get stuffed!"

The police officer closed the door as Ellie Marshall swung around and smiled at the camera.

"That's right Angela. You heard it first. Omnibank has admitted to its shareholders and the Australian public that they can all get stuffed!"

****

In the Prime Ministers Office in Canberra, the Prime Minister switched off the television footage of Ellie Marshall and Angela Kostakos.

"Shit," said Marion Alright as there was a knock at the door and two Federal Police Officers entered.

"Marion Alright?" said the first Federal Police Officer.

"Shit," said Marion Alright.

****

In the hospital emergency ward, Kate was sitting next to Bart Manning, sleeping in a bed, with monitors hooked up to him. Her phone rang. She looked at the caller and it was Percy. She let it go to voice mail.

"You should really give him a break," said Bart Manning softly.

Kate was startled at first before turning around to see Bart was awake. She reached over to hold his hand.

"You are awake! Thank goodness. How did you know?"

Bart Manning coughed. "I glanced his name on your phone-"

Bart Manning coughed again.

"Do you want me to get the nurse?" asked Kate.

Bart Manning waved negatively and pointed to a glass of water on the table. Kate handed it to him and he sipped a few times before resting his head back on his pillow.

"The fool doth think he is wise, but the wise man knows himself to be a fool, my dear. "

Kate shook her head. "Always riddles you lawyers. I never understand."

"Percy is a good soul, like you Kate."

Kate smiled as her phone rang again and this time it was her son Ben. She picked up.

"Ben, honey. Is everything OK? How is Rex?"

****

Inside the kitchen of Kates House, Ben was on the phone as Sophie was tearing up the evidence of a pizza box.

"He is still depressed. So I put him out the back with some of Percy's old clothes and he is sleeping. We're going to go and see Percy."

"Don't ride your motor bike at night. You know how dangerous it is."

Ben made faces.

"Yes mum."

****

A young doctor and nurse came up to the bed, while Kate was still on the phone. The Doctor pulled the chart from the front of the bed, before smiling at Kate.

"I've got to go honey," said Kate. "You be safe. Love you."

"Yes mum."

Kate hung up the phone as the doctor stepped over and started to examine Bart Manning.

"Is he going to be OK?" asked Kate.

"He suffered a mild hyper glycemic seizure," replied the doctor. "Apart from the fact that his liver is shot from excessive alcohol consumption, he should be OK."

"I am not an inanimate object young man," grumbled Bart Manning. "When can I depart this infernal place of dread?"

The doctor stepped back. "In a few days. "

"A few days! We do not have a few days!"

Bart Manning sat up in bed looking agitated as the nurse rushed over to help the Doctor calm him down.

"Calm down Mr Manning. We don't want you to have a stroke."

Kates phone rang again. She looked down at the caller ID. It was Percy. This time she accepted the call.

****

Inside the police station, Percy was now out of the cell and sitting with Jagamara having some take away dinner.

"Hi. It's me," said Percy.

"Hi," said Kate without emotion.

"I am still with Jagamara till the morning. But I should be released tomorrow."

"The kids want to come and see you," said Kate. "I told Ben not to ride his motor bike."

Percy smiled.

"How is Bart? I heard about him going to hospital. "

****

59

The Doctor nodded and started to walk away with the Nurse.

"Look Percy. I have to go."

"I do love you, Miss Kate -"

Kate clicked off the phone before Percy had finished. Bart Manning reached out and touched the arm of Kate.

"It will be fine, my dear."

Kate wiped her face as tears started to well up.

"What will I do in court tomorrow?"

Bart Manning smiled.

"You are loved. You are surrounded by love. So you have nothing to fear."

Chapter 13

It was night time as Victor and Lewis were watching the Kate's House from the blue van. They saw Ben leave on a motor bike, before getting out of the van and scurrying over to the side of the house.

By the side of the house, Lewis Botta ran into the tin bin making a loud sound, causing Rex to bark outside.

"Careful," grumbled Victor, before both men slip into the house through the kitchen door.

****

Upstairs in Kate's House, Sophie had her ear phones in and was on the computer. She was interacting on social media and oblivious to the sounds below.

****

Ben parked his motor bike out the front of the police station. Inside, Sgt. Jagamara and then Percy greet him.

"Your mum is going to kill you riding that thing," said Percy.

Ben shrugged his shoulders and smiled.

"She only wants you to be safe," said Sgt. Jagamara. "You should come out with me one weekend, to see what it is like on the roads."

"No thanks Jagamara," replied Ben. "But I do drive safe and wear a helmet."

"Do you wear a helmet?" added Percy. "That's better than me."

Sgt. Jagamara gave Percy a deadpan stare.

****

Lewis Botta and Victor continued rummaging through the kitchen, opening cupboards and drawers. Victor pointed to the exit into the dining room.

"You go," he whispered. "You go in there."

Lewis Botta stepped into the dining room as Victor continued to go through the kitchen drawers. But when he got to the cutlery drawer, he opened it too far and the whole contents of knives, forks and spoons came crashing down onto the kitchen floor.

****

Sophie heard the crash even through her ear phones.

"Stop playing your video games so loud Ben!" she yelled

There was no response. Sophie got up from her chair and stepped into the upstairs hallway and stairs. When she was at the top of the stairs, she could see the house lights were off, and two torches were flickering below.

Sophie crouched down at the stairs and watched the torch lights as they flashed across the walls. One beam narrowly missed her crouching on the stairs.

She put her hands to her mouth in absolute fright and slowly reversed back into her room.

Victor entered the Dining Room to find that Lewis Botta had cut open all the cushions creating a complete shambles. Victor shook his head.

"What are you doing?"

"I am looking at all the possible hiding places," said Lewis Botta

Sophie hid behind her bed and dialled her phone.

****

In the Hospital Emergency ward, Kate was half asleep, next to a sleeping Bart Manning when her phone started ringing.

"Sophie honey. Is everything OK?"

"Mom. There is someone in our house," said Sophie in complete panic.

Kate's face was one of horror and shock.

"Sophie get off the phone and hide OK. Jagamara will be over there soon honey. OK?"

"OK mom. Please hurry."

Kate hung up and looked down at her phone and dialled Percy back.

****

Jagamara and Ben were laughing as Percy looked at the phone.

"It's your mom."

Ben waves at Percy.

"Don't tell mum I took the bike."

Percy nodded as he took the call and put it on speaker phone.

"Hi Kate, Ben is here -"

"Percy, someone is at the house," said Kate, interrupting Percy.

Percy, Jagamara and Ben all stop smiling.

"Sophie is petrified," said Kate. "Get Jagamara over their right now and help my little baby."

"I'm here Kate," said Sgt. Jagamara. "We're on our way."

Kate hung up the phone, as Percy, Sgt. Jagamara and Ben get up and leave. Outside, Sgt. Jagamara unlocks the police car and they all get in.

"Hey Percy," said Sgt. Jagamara. "Remember, you are still technically a prisoner of the state."

"No problem," said Percy. "Then handcuff me to the door. But lets go. Sophie is in trouble."

Jagamara started the police car, spun it around and sped off, lights flashing.

****

The Dining Room was a complete mess. Even some of the pictures thrown down onto the ground were broken. Outside, Rex continued to bark in the background.

"It is not here," grumbled Victor.

"Maybe the caravan out the back?" said Lewis Botta.

Victor stepped out of the room, followed by Lewis Botta. Victor opened the back door to a barking Rex, with Lewis looking less than comfortable. There was no caravan in site.

"Nice doggie," said Lewis Botta.

"Kill it."

Lewis Botta looked at Victor with a look of disgust. "What kind of monster are you? This is a beautiful dog."

"Then we will take him for ransom," said Victor as he sneezed.

Victor untied Rex and then started to try and drag Rex into the house, while Rex resisted. Victor sneezed again.

Chapter 14

The Police Car of Sgt. Jagamara sped past the blue van driven by Victor with Lewis Botta on the road to Kate's house.

When they got to Kate's House, Sophie was already standing outside, being consoled by Mary-Ann McNamara. Percy, Sgt. Jagamara and Ben jump out of the police car and run over to her.

"They took Rex," sobbed Sophie.

Sgt. Jagamara looked over at Percy. He looked in a state of shock. Sgt. Jagamara grabbed his arm to shake him out of it, dragging him back toward the police car.

"Call your mum and tell her Sophie is safe," said Sgt. Jagamara to Ben. "We gotta go after these dog stealing fellas."

Ben pulled out his phone, as Sgt. Jagamara bundled Percy into the police car and sped off.

"How are you going to track them at night?" asked Percy, as the police car barrelled back toward the main street.

Sgt. Jagamara smiled. "I reckon that blue van is the one."

"Get on your phone Percy. Wake up the town. We are going to find these fellas and get Rex back."

****

Victor pulled his blue van up outside Percy's Caravan that was dumped at the Headland reserve. Someone had spray painted DIE SCUM and ARSEHOLE in big letters across it. Victor and Lewis got out of the van, with Rex tied up in the back of the van.

At the same time Sgt Jagamara continued to drive at speed, with the police lights flashing down the road leaving Eelang. Percy continued to send messages to the town.

"OK, I've got most the town up, said Percy. Koz is on the road and looking; and the fishermen will be on the road in a sec."

"If they'd left the town we would have caught them by now. I think they're still here."

Sgt. Jagamara stopped the police car abruptly and spun it around.

"Tell everyone to be on the look out," said Sgt. Jagamara. "The van must be somewhere."

"Where did Kate tow my caravan?"

****

Inside the caravan, Lewis and Victor continue trashing the interior looking for the patent.

"It is not here," moaned Victor.

"Can we burn it?" asked Lewis Botta.

Victor slaps his forehead in frustration.

****

Percy and Sgt. Jagamara speed toward the location of the caravan when Percy's phone started to ring.

"Hello?" said Percy. "Right. OK I'll tell him."

"What?"

"Everyone is up," smiled Percy.

"OK. Tell them not to move and make sure there is no exit. I don't want these rats slipping away," said Sgt. Jagamara.

"Jagamara says no one move and make sure the exit is blocked." Percy hung up the phone.

****

Victor and Lewis Botta leave the headland, with the Caravan well alight.

Percy and Sgt. Jagamara just arrived from the other end to see the Caravan was alight.

Percy got out of the police car and rushed to the caravan on fire.

"Rex! Rex!" he yelled

"He's not here," said Sgt. Jagamara "Trust me. We'll get them, we will get Rex back."

Percy bowed his head for a second at the site of his caravan burning to the ground. Sgt. Jagamara looked in the distance and saw the distinct break lights of the van making a turn.

"There they are!"

Percy jumped back into the police car and Sgt. Jagamara puts the police siren and lights back on. Percy's phone rang. he picked it up.

"Yep the blue van is coming up on you now. We are behind them," he said before he hung up the phone.

The blue van of Victor turned onto the main street of Eelang to be confronted with a wall of blinding lights from the headlights of cars and trucks. Victor stops the van for a moment.

"What do we do? The Police are behind us."

Lewis Botta looked over as Victor finally produces a handgun from under the seat.

"Oh no," said Lewis Botta. "I am not going to prison."

Lewis instinctively opened up the passenger door and jumped out of the vehicle. Before Victor can accelerate away, the driver's door swung open and Vivien Li karate chopped him. Victor fell out onto the road, with Vivian Li kicking the handgun clear and then standing on his chest.

"No one threatens my town," she said.

The Police Car pulled up behind the van and Percy rushed out and opened up the back to untie and release Rex. As soon as Rex saw Percy, he started to give him licks.

"Good boy Rex. I missed you!"

Sgt. Jagamara, aided by Vivien Li hand cuff Victor and Lewis Botta and put them in the back of his police car.

Chapter 15

Inside the courtroom, Kate was standing on her own. Next to her was Wade Pemberton, looking cocky and self assured.

"You can't win," he sneered.

"Excuse me?" said Kate, pretending she hadn't heard him.

"The banks always win," grinned Wade Pemberton.

Kate looked straight ahead, as everyone stood on the arrival of Justice Peters into the court.

"We will see about that, won't we," whispered Kate.

Everyone sat back down.

"Miss Lang," said the judge. "I note that you have asked to be recognised as an Agent to the Defence and not seek the aide of temporary counsel."

Kate nodded.

"Yes your honour."

"Very well," continued Justice Peters, "as counsel has been taken ill and the parties have presented their final evidence, I will not be hearing any more testimony or arguments. However, I remind the defence that I am yet to see a copy of the land patent to which Bart Manning referred and if it is not produced to the court by close of business today, then I am afraid I will have to rule in favour of the plaintiff."

The judge rose and bowed, leaving Kate in shock as Wade Pemberton beamed.

"Good luck with your packing Miss Lang," he sniggered.

****

Inside Kate's House, Percy was helping to clean up the house along with the kids. Sgt. Jagamara was there too, writing his paperwork, with his phone on speaker, as he was speaking with Kate.

"What do I do?" she asked.

"What can you do but be strong and hope for a miracle," said Sgt. Jagamara.

Percy stepped into the Dining Room. He shook his head at the mess as he moved over to the damaged portrait of Charles E. Lang.

"I am sorry Charles E. I really stuffed up this time."

Percy tried to push the frame back together, but it was obstructed by something that has slid down between the canvas and the backing of the picture. Percy turned over the canvas and looked. He saw the edge of an old looking document and an official British Government crest. Quickly he tore off the brown paper backing to the portrait to reveal the land patent.

"I've found it!" he yelled.

Percy bounded into the kitchen, holding the land patent and almost bowled over Sgt. Jagamara.

"I've found it!" yelled Percy again.

Sgt Jagamara looked at the document and his face beamed.

"You beauty!"

"What, what is going on?" asked Kate. Percy picked up the phone

"I found it Kate. I found the land patent."

"Oh Percy! But how can we get it down here in time? There is only a few hours before I have to go back to court. If it is not here, then it is all over."

"Don't you worry Miss Kate. Sergeant Jagamara is on the case. We'll be there before you can say Constitutional Recognition."

****

Inside the courtroom, Kate was standing anxiously as Justice Peters re-entered.

"Well Miss Lang?" as the judge.

"Your Honour, the land patent is on its way," she smiled as Wade Pemberton darted a look of alarm.

"How long Miss Lang?" asked Justice Peters.

"Any minute, your Honour."

"I object," yelled Wade Pemberton. "She lacks sufficient standing to introduce such new evidence."

The judge shook his head before looking back at Wade Pemberton.

"Go on," said the judge.

"Miss Lang claims to hold powers of attorney in fact or agent for the Defence, yet I have not been provided a copy of any letter of authority or appearance tendered to the court."

Justice Peters bowed his head. "I am afraid counsel is correct. Even if the document you say does arrive in the next few minutes, you do not have sufficient standing on record for the court to accept your submission."

"You are a judge," said Kate frustratingly. "Can't you grant some kind of special dispensation?"

Justice Peters shrugged his shoulders as Wade Pemberton had a smug look of arrogant superiority on his face.

"The law is always right Miss Lang," said the judge.

"Maybe I can be of some assistance to my psychic and all knowing colleague?" said a voice from the back of the court.

Everyone turned around to see the figure of Bart Manning dressed in hospital gown and slippers. Holding the land patent in one hand, while wheeling a drip on a trolley on the other. Accompanied by Percy and Sgt. Jagamara.

The face of Wade Pemberton transformed from white to then red.

"And in case my omnipotent colleague wishes to waste any more of the court's time concerning appearances, I remain, at present, in the official state issued attire of the Government Hospital Service."

Kate was beaming as Bart Manning wheels himself past and handed the land patent to the clerk. Kate rushed forward and kissed him.

"If chance will have me king, why, chance may crown me," smiled Bart Manning. "Shakespeare dear boy."

Kate turned to Percy and rushed up and hugged him before they kiss passionately.

****

A new day on the main street of Eelang. In the window of the shop named *Kingdom Of Eelang Souvenirs And Post Office* was a large decorative plate, for the price tag of 99 dollars. It showed an imprinted picture of Percy, Kate, Sophie and Ben and Rex in a portrait shot, with the words *Royal Family Of The Kingdom Of Eelang* at the bottom of it.

King and Country

www.ingramcontent.com/pod-product-compliance
Lightning Source LLC
Chambersburg PA
CBHW082250120626
46555CB00009B/3025